The Daring Rescue of
Marlon the
Swimming Pig

By Susan Saunders
Illustrated by Gail Owens

A STEPPING STONE BOOK

Random House New York

For Stephanie, who appreciates pigs

Library of Congress Cataloging-in-Publication Data:
Saunders, Susan. The daring rescue of Marlon the swimming pig. (A Stepping stone book) SUMMARY: Two young boys get more than they bargained for when they try to save the swimming pig star of the local Aquarama from being sent to slaughter. [1. Pigs—Fiction] I. Owens, Gail, ill. II. Title. III. Series: Stepping stone book (Random House (Firm)) PZ7.S2577Dar 1987 [Fic] 87-4633 ISBN: 0-394-88293-8 (pbk.); 0-394-98293-2 (lib. bdg.)

Manufactured in the United States of America   4 5 6 7 8 9 0

Contents

1
The Star of the Aquarama

He stood straight and tall at the end of the diving board, muscles rippling under his smooth skin. He gazed serenely at the hushed audience to his right and to his left. Then he lifted his proud head, took a deep breath, and dove neatly into the pool. His body cut through the ice-cold water like a knife—there was hardly a splash. He bobbed to the surface to lively applause and swam to the pool's edge.

"He's looking good today," said Hartley Schroeder with a satisfied nod. "I'll bet Marlon dives the best of any pig in the country." Hartley was sitting in the cypress tree on the crest of the hill with his best friend, Justin Jones.

Hartley was a stocky, cheerful-looking boy with straight brown hair. Justin was a little taller and thinner. Both of them leaned forward expectantly, staring down at the pool below them.

"Time for the drowning part," Justin announced.

"Yeah—there's Donna," Hartley said.

A young woman wearing a flowered shirt and shorts lowered herself into the water. She paddled slowly to the center of the pool. Suddenly she began to flounder and thrash about. "Help!" Donna shrieked. "Help! Save me!"

"Oh!" gasped the people in the bleachers. Several rose anxiously to their feet.

The heroic Marlon, brown ears pricked, was already galloping around the pool. Without even pausing, he flung himself forward in a racing dive. His short but powerful legs churned the deep-blue water into a white froth as he swam gallantly to the young woman's aid.

"Donna says the only bad thing is getting pinched sometimes when Marlon grabs hold of her," Hartley reported. Donna was Hartley's brother's girlfriend, and an Aquarama mermaid.

Avoiding Donna's thrashing arms and legs, Marlon took a firm grip with his teeth on the back of her shirt. Then, like a tugboat maneuvering an unruly freighter, he steered her safely to shore.

Marlon and Donna scrambled out of the pool to wild applause. Donna rewarded her rescuer with a big slice of watermelon, which he gulped down in two bites.

"That's it—show's over," Justin declared.

The show was the Cedar Springs Aquarama, and Marlon was its star performer. From their perch, the boys could see only half the show, however.

The first half took place underground. "I wouldn't pay three cents to see it," Hartley had often said disdainfully. But it would actually take two dollars and fifty cents if you wanted to buy a ticket to the underground auditorium, the low, flat-roofed building at one end of the pool. Once inside and down the steps, you'd sit in front of a big glass window stretching from floor to ceiling and from wall to wall.

The clear spring water of the pool was on the other side of the window—it percolated up from deep in the earth. On the white sand at the bottom of the pool lay six enormous clamshells.

The lights of the underground auditorium would dim, and what Hartley called goopy music would fill the room. Slowly, slowly, the giant clamshells would open. A young woman in a gleaming bathing suit and matching cap would uncurl from each of the shells, surrounded by silvery bubbles.

Then the six young women—the Aquarama Mermaids—would perform an underwater ballet, smiling blindly through the glass at their audience. They would flip and spin and twirl to the music, stopping now and then to take a breath from one of the air hoses hidden among strands of plastic seaweed.

The whole thing, Hartley said, was dumb. "Giant clams don't grow in fresh water, much less have *girls* inside them!"

It was only when the water ballet was over—and the young women tucked back into their clams—that the audience would troop up the steps to see Marlon.

Marlon the swimming pig was the most famous citizen of Cedar Springs. He was known all over the state. He'd even been in *U.S.* magazine: "Swimming pig packs them in like sardines," with a picture of Marlon in front of a large and enthusiastic audience.

Until recently Justin and Hartley had only seen Marlon perform a few times—usually when out-of-town visitors asked to be taken to the Aquarama. This summer, however, Hartley's family had moved across town to a white frame house on top of the hill. Soon Hartley discovered that from high in the cypress tree he could see over all the cedars blanketing the hill's lower slopes, straight down into the Aquarama pool.

Right away, Hartley and Justin carried some scrap lumber up into the tree. They nailed down a few boards to make a comfortable balcony seat. When it was done, they could watch Marlon dive as many times as they liked.

After three days of watching him, Hartley wanted to take a closer look at the star of the show. The boys happened to have some chocolate chip cookies in their pockets when they climbed down the hill that first time. They offered a cookie to Marlon to get him to come closer to the wire fence. Naturally one cookie led to another, and by the end of the visit the three of them were becoming fast friends.

From that time on, Hartley and Justin had visited Marlon almost every day, as soon as the afternoon show was over. Now the boys were waiting until the crowd had climbed down from the bleachers and headed to their cars.

"That's the last one," Hartley said. "Let's go."

2
A Visit
to a Friend

Hartley lowered himself down a few branches. Then he swung out of the tree and dropped to the ground. When Justin landed with a thud beside him, Hartley said, "Mom gave me some squashy tomatoes, peppers with holes in them, two rotten cantaloupes, and other junk from the garden. What did you bring?"

Justin looked into the paper bag he had propped against the bottom of the cypress. "Three family-sized loaves of bread that were getting too old, some cans of green beans—dented, and two jars of spiced peaches that leaked."

Justin's father owned the Handy Dandy, the biggest grocery store in Cedar Springs. Whatever he was going to throw out these days went to Marlon instead—the pig wasn't as particular as Mr. Jones's customers.

Hartley lifted his cardboard box of vegetables off the back steps of the house. Justin picked up his paper bag. The two of them walked to the edge of the hill and down the far side. They had made this trip so many times already that they had worn a narrow path through the weeds growing beneath the cedar trees.

Hartley and Justin weren't halfway down the hill when they were greeted by a long, drawn-out squeal. "He hears us coming," Hartley said with a grin.

The squeal was followed by insistent grunts that grew louder and faster as the boys got closer. Hartley and Justin squeezed between the trees in the last clump of cedars, and stepped out into the cleared space next to the Aquarama fence.

They were welcomed with explosive snorts by a fine-looking brown pig, a little over two feet tall at the shoulder, with a single white spot on his left side. He had soft brown eyes, large pointed ears, and a mouth that turned up at the corners. Marlon wriggled gleefully and pressed his snout against the wire-mesh fence.

The six-foot fence enclosed all of the Aquarama grounds. Marlon's pen was at the back. He had a sleeping shed, a water bucket, and a long metal trough to eat out of. Past the pen was the rock pool with the diving board. The flat-roofed auditorium stood at the end of the pool.

"Hey, Marlon!" Hartley said, setting down the box of vegetables and rubbing the pig's wet nose. "What's happening?"

"We've got some good stuff for you today," Justin added, putting his paper bag on the ground next to the fence.

Marlon started to trot around and around in a circle, huffing and grunting impatiently.

Justin pulled a package of bread out of the bag and tore it open. He pitched it over the wire-mesh fence by the handful. Although Marlon's trough was half filled with pig feed, he fell on the bread as though he hadn't eaten in weeks. He had barely stuffed it down when Hartley tossed over the two cantaloupes. They hit the ground on the other side of the fence with a *splat!* and cracked wide open. With a blissful shriek, Marlon chomped his way quickly through both of them.

"Look at that smile," said Hartley fondly.

Marlon kept the boys busy, grunting his encouragement as they threw in more bread, followed immediately by tomatoes and peppers. Then Justin pried open some cans of green beans with his Scout knife. Hartley poured them through the fence as fast as he could, to squeals of delight from the pig.

"Let's save the spiced peaches for his dessert," Hartley suggested.

Justin nodded. "Uh-oh, here comes Mr. Albright," he muttered suddenly. Justin straightened up and stared nervously at the large, gray-haired man in the white cowboy hat who was standing at the auditorium door.

Gus Albright owned the Aquarama. He owned Marlon, too, and Hartley and Justin had never asked his permission to feed the pig.

"What are you worrying about? We're not doing anything wrong," Hartley told Justin. "Pigs are *supposed* to eat."

Mr. Albright seemed to agree. He gave them a big wave and called out, "Hey there, boys—enjoy yourselves!"

They watched him stride across the grass to the front gate. Mr. Albright locked the gate with a large padlock before driving away in his shiny white Cadillac.

Hartley and Justin hurled the remaining tomatoes, a big, wrinkled squash, and the rest of the stale bread over the fence. They poured out the last two cans of beans for Marlon. Then the boys dug into the jars of spiced peaches with their fingers.

They took turns squeezing peaches through the wire mesh. Marlon plucked the fruit carefully from their fingers. He swallowed the peaches with satisfied sighs, pits and all.

"No more," Hartley told Marlon, wiping his sticky hands on his jeans.

The boys sat down to rest on their side of the fence. Marlon lay down companionably on the other side, right next to the wire, so they could reach his broad back.

Hartley and Justin scratched Marlon's back through the fence and talked to him, just keeping him company, until the sun began to drop behind the hill.

"I'd better go," Justin said then. "I've got to pick up my bike and get home for supper."

As the boys climbed to their feet, Marlon did too. His shining eyes seemed to beam his affection. His lips curled up charmingly.

"See you tomorrow," Hartley called to the pig as they started up the hill.

"*Sno-o-rrt*," Marlon answered, his short tail spinning.

3
The Awful Truth About Marlon

Hap was waxing his blue pickup truck in the Schroeders' driveway when Hartley and Justin walked around to the front of the house. Hap was Hartley's brother—he was eighteen years old. Next came fifteen-year-old Katie. Hartley was the youngest at ten and a half.

Carefully Hap wiped a few drops of wax off the right front fender. He glanced up from his work to ask, "Where have you two been—still helping Gus Albright fatten up the pig for Paleyville?"

"Paleyville?" Hartley repeated, looking puzzled.

"The Paleyville auction," Hap said, stooping to polish the chrome on the bumper. "Isn't it about time for Marlon to go to the auction?"

Hartley and Justin stared at each other. Gus Albright wouldn't send Marlon to the auction! Make sausage of the best swimming pig in the country? He couldn't!

"What's that supposed to mean?" Hartley demanded. "Are you trying to be funny or something?"

"That pig must weigh about three hundred pounds now," Hap said, his mind still on his truck and not on his little brother. "Everybody knows Gus doesn't keep them much past that—it doesn't make good business sense."

Hap stepped back to admire the sheen on his hood. "Donna's already been working with the new pig for a couple of weeks, out at Gus's farm," Hap added. "It should be just about ready."

"Wh-what new pig?" Justin stammered when he got excited.

"The new diving Marlon," Hap answered, reaching out to straighten the radio antenna on his truck. "*This* Marlon's replacement. Pigs learn real fast—Gus trains a new one every year."

The boys were dumbstruck. *Every year?*

"You m-mean this year's Marlon is different from last year's?" Justin said finally.

"Sure. Last year's, and the year before

that, and the year before that," Hap said. "I thought you guys knew." He stroked the truck's headlights with a rag.

"But I've been seeing the same Marlon all my life," Hartley argued.

"You've been seeing a brown pig with a white spot," his brother told him. "How many brown, spotted pigs are there? Probably millions." Hap went on, "Think about it. How big do pigs get?"

"Real big," Hartley admitted. His great-uncle Bill had had a pig named Beevo that weighed twelve hundred pounds and stood as high as his chest.

"Haven't you ever wondered why Marlon doesn't get any bigger?" Hap asked the two boys. "A full-grown pig usually weighs somewhere around a thousand pounds. It'd cost a fortune just to feed him. Plus which, if a thousand-pound pig jumped into that little pool at the Aquarama, there wouldn't be any water left in it!" He laughed. "No room for Donna, either."

Hap snapped the top closed on the plastic bottle of wax and took a good look at the boys' horrified faces at last. "Come on," he said, trying to cheer them up, "you'll like the new pig."

Hap collected the rags he'd used to polish his truck. Then he bounded up the front steps and, whistling to himself, disappeared inside the house.

The boys were silent for a minute or two. Neither of them wanted to believe it about Marlon, but they knew Hap wouldn't lie just to be mean.

"It's like finding out there's no Santa Claus," Hartley said slowly. "There's not much left to believe in."

Justin nodded solemnly. "I don't think I'll bring anything from the store tomorrow," he told Hartley. "Doesn't seem to be any point to it."

After Justin had ridden away on his bike, Hartley shinnied up the cypress tree again. The setting sun had turned the sky a bright orange. Down at the bottom of the hill, bathed in a golden glow, lay Marlon the swimming pig. He was sprawled out flat on his side—his brown legs twitching now and then—having happy pig dreams.

Hartley felt sick.

4
Hartley Loses His Appetite

Hartley didn't eat much for supper that night. His mother had cooked his favorite—chicken and dumplings—but Hartley could barely finish one dumpling. He didn't join in the conversation, either.

"What's the matter with Hartley?" Mr. Schroeder asked Mrs. Schroeder in a low voice. "It's not like him to be so quiet."

She shook her head and looked concerned.

"I think it's the pig," Hap volunteered.

"What pig?" asked his father.

"Marlon, the pig at the Aquarama."

"What about him?" Katie asked.

"Hartley didn't know about Marlon going to the Paleyville auction," Hap murmured.

"Oh," said Mr. Schroeder.

The whole family stared at Hartley.

"I'm not hungry," he said abruptly. "Can I be excused?"

When his mother said yes, Hartley pushed back his chair and walked quickly through the kitchen to the screen door. He pushed it open and flopped down on the back steps, squinting up at the moon.

Before long he heard the screen door creak open and his father joined him outside.

"You okay, Son?" Mr. Schroeder asked.

"How much does a pig cost?" Hartley wanted to know.

"Well—I think they're getting about sixty cents a pound for pigs right now," his father answered.

Sixty cents a pound times three hundred pounds . . . Hartley tried to figure it out in his head. He wasn't certain of the total, but he knew it came to a lot more than the eight dollars he had saved from his last birthday. Hartley sighed.

"Do you want to talk about anything?" his father asked him.

Hartley shook his head. Mr. Schroeder patted him on the shoulder and went back inside the house.

With his finger, Hartley wrote $300 \times .60$

in the dirt at the bottom of the steps. One hundred eighty dollars! He rubbed it out with his sneaker and sighed again. Probably not even his father had that much money saved — at least, not to spend on a pig.

The livestock auction was held every Friday in Paleyville. If Gus Albright meant to take Marlon this Friday . . . it was only four days away!

Hartley thought about Marlon. He thought about his warm brown eyes and his mouth that curled up in a smile. He thought of the way Marlon squealed a hello when he heard the boys coming down the hill to visit. Marlon was really more like a person than an animal. In fact, after Justin, Marlon was Hartley's best friend.

If Justin were in trouble, could he turn his back on him? Of course not. And Hartley wouldn't turn his back on Marlon, either.

He couldn't afford to buy the pig, and Mr. Albright certainly wasn't going to give Marlon away for free. In four days, Marlon could be gone forever. There was only one thing left to do!

5
The Plan

"*S-steal Marlon?*" Justin exclaimed.

"Sssh! Keep it down!" Hartley warned, looking around to see if anyone was within earshot. Luckily, Main Street in Cedar Springs was pretty empty at eight o'clock in the morning. "It's more like rescuing a friend from certain death," he told Justin in a low voice.

"How do you figure we could get him out of the Aquarama, anyway?" Justin muttered discouragingly. "Mr. Albright always locks the gate at night. Marlon can do lots of things, but he can't jump over a six-foot wire fence, or climb it, either."

"I've already thought of that," Hartley said briskly. "My dad keeps some wire cutters in his van that will slice through *iron*." Mr. Schroeder was an electrician.

Justin groaned. Not only was Hartley planning to steal a pig—he was going to cut up a fence to do it! "Well, if we *could* get him out, what would we do with him?" Justin asked, hoping Hartley would come to his senses. "A three-hundred-pound pig isn't exactly invisible."

"I've thought of that, too," Hartley answered promptly. "You know the old Thompson place?"

"Past the railroad tracks," said Justin.

"Right. Nobody's lived in the house for ages. Hap took me down there once to catch some frogs for science class at the high school—the creek runs in back of the house. And I remember seeing a wood pen and an old shed on the other side of the creek," said Hartley. "It'll be just right for Marlon."

"I don't know," Justin said gloomily. "What if we get caught? There are three of you—"

"I know," Hartley interrupted. "And only one of you."

Whenever Hartley came up with one of his plans, Justin always said the same thing: "If we get caught, *I'll* get in worse trouble. There are three kids in your family for your parents to dump on, so everybody gets less of it. In my family there's just me—and I get it all."

"Anyway, we're not going to get caught," Hartley assured his friend.

"Justin, have you finished sweeping that sidewalk?" Mr. Jones called from inside the Handy Dandy. In the summertime, Justin always helped open up the grocery in the morning.

"I'm just about done," Justin answered his father, grabbing the broom and sweeping absent-mindedly.

"Justin," Hartley said sternly, "in a week Marlon could be nothing more than a hundred packages of plastic-wrapped bacon!"

Justin stopped sweeping again. He looked at Hartley.

"He's our friend. Are you with me or not?" Hartley asked.

"I guess so," Justin mumbled.

"Good," Hartley said with a triumphant grin. "Come to my house this afternoon, and we'll go over the plan."

"I can't," said Justin. "This afternoon

Mom is taking me to visit Aunt Minnie in Artesia."

"Then I'll just explain as we go along," Hartley decided. "We'll meet at the cypress tree at midnight tonight."

"Midnight?" Justin protested. "How'm I supposed to get out of the house without somebody hearing? My parents will kill me!"

"You can do it," Hartley said. "Bring lots of cookies with you when you come."

"Justin!" Mr. Jones called again.

"See you tonight," Hartley said as he climbed onto his bike.

Hartley worked hard that day. His first stop was the old Thompson place. The house stood alone at the end of a curving dirt road. It was a big wooden two-story, unpainted for so long that it had turned a dreary grayish brown. Most of the window panes were broken. The front door hung crookedly open, the top hinge pulling loose from the frame.

"Spooky," Hartley said to himself. "That's good—nobody'll come poking around here."

He dragged his bike past the house to the back. He leaned it against the porch and walked through the overgrown backyard.

The narrow bridge of planks that crossed Cullen Creek had fallen down years before. Since the creek was almost dry this summer, it didn't matter—Hartley could walk right on the creek bed.

But the wooden pen around the shed was very rickety. One of the upright posts was half eaten by termites, and some of the boards were missing.

"Marlon could push this fence over just scratching his back on it," Hartley said to himself.

He rode home for supplies: a hammer and nails, wire, even the boards from the perch in the cypress tree. By the middle of the afternoon he was finished. He had wired and nailed the pen back together and filled an old metal bucket with water from a puddle in the creek bed.

"This'll do fine," he said proudly.

Hartley was home in time to watch Marlon's last dive of the afternoon. The pig posed on the diving board for a moment. Then his brown body arched gracefully through the air, the sun winking off his white spot. The people in the bleachers clapped loudly. There was even some whistling and foot stomping.

"I'm afraid you won't be a star anymore, Marlon. But you're not going to be bacon, either," Hartley promised from high up in the cypress tree.

At supper that night Mr. Schroeder said, "I know what Hap did this afternoon." Hap had a summer job with the highway department. "What about you two?"

"A bunch of us went swimming in Carol's pool," Katie told him.

"Hartley?" prompted Mrs. Schroeder.

"Uh—nothing much," Hartley answered, helping himself to another slice of meat loaf. Now that he'd planned how to save Marlon, his appetite had come back.

"Didn't I see you on the dirt road near the old Thompson place with some boards?" Hap asked.

Hartley almost dropped his fork. "That wasn't me," he said stiffly. Older brothers could really be a drag!

Hap wasn't interested enough to pursue it, though. "Guess it was some other kid on a bike," he said, before going on to tell his father about how he'd driven a bulldozer that day.

Close call, Hartley thought. He didn't want the Thompson place on anyone's mind right now.

After supper Hartley slipped into the van to find his father's wire cutters. A flashlight from the hall closet completed his rescue kit.

"I'm kind of tired," Hartley announced to his parents at nine thirty. "I'm going to bed."

He closed the door to his bedroom. He pulled off his sneakers, but he left his clothes on. Before Hartley turned out the light, he moved the clock so that he could see the face clearly. Then he climbed into bed. He pulled the sheets up under his chin, just in case someone looked in.

Hartley watched the glowing minute hand move around the clock face. At ten o'clock his parents switched off the television and went to bed. At ten thirty Katie turned off her tape player. At eleven Hartley heard Hap's truck pull up in the driveway—he was back from a friend's house.

Hartley's eyes felt heavier and heavier. He closed them for just a minute.

Scritch, scritch. Hartley sat up with a start and looked at the clock. It was ten after twelve. *Scritch.*

"Hartley!" Justin whispered. He'd been scratching on the screen of Hartley's window. "Are you sleeping?"

"Of course not," Hartley answered.

He pulled on his sneakers, stuffed the wire cutters in his back pocket, and opened the screen. Grabbing the flashlight, he crawled out the window and into the night.

6
Home Safe

"I've been waiting for you at the cypress!" Justin complained indignantly.

"Sorry—I must've lost track of time," Hartley told him. Then he took charge. "Did you bring the cookies?"

"Two bags of chocolate chips," Justin answered. "They're under the tree."

The moon was shining so brightly that it cast shadows on the lawn. The boys grabbed the cookies and started down the side of the hill. Suddenly the cedar trees loomed over them from all sides.

"B-boy, it's sure dark under these cedars," said Justin. The wind rustled the dry weeds.

Hartley switched on the flashlight. "It's just like it is in the daytime," he told Justin reprovingly, "only it's night." His mind was on what lay ahead.

When the boys stepped out of the trees and into the moonlight again, there was no greeting from Marlon. He was sleeping soundly. They could hear deep, rumbly snores coming from the far side of the pen.

"Marlon!" Hartley whispered. He shone the flashlight on the smooth brown body.

There was a startled snort with a question mark at the end of it.

"It's us!" Hartley said reassuringly.

Marlon scrambled to his feet and trotted eagerly to the back fence, grunting and huffing a welcome. The boys were a little late in bringing him his treats today, so he was especially glad to see them.

"Give him a cookie, just to get him to pay attention," Hartley directed. "Only one."

While Justin tore open a bag, Hartley pulled the wire cutters out of his back pocket. He stuck the flashlight under one arm and used both hands. *Snick.* The cutters sliced smoothly through a strand of wire mesh.

"This is easy," Hartley whispered.

All of a sudden there was a ferocious growl from somewhere near the auditorium!

Hartley grabbed the flashlight and swung it around. Two big eyes and a set of sharp white fangs gleamed in the beam of light.

"It's a w-wolf!" Justin stammered. "It's coming closer!"

The flashlight shook in Hartley's hand. He managed to hold it steady enough to pick out a broad flat nose and droopy ears. "It's a dog," Hartley said, breathing easier. "Gus Albright must put a watchdog in here at night. Remember when somebody climbed the fence and dumped soap into the pool?" The next morning the pool had looked like a giant bubble bath. "He doesn't want that to happen again."

The watchdog began to bark—loudly, piercingly, and repeatedly.

Hartley went back to snipping the fence. "He can't get to us. Marlon's pen is in the way."

"But he's going to wake up everybody in town!" Justin pointed out.

Hartley quit snipping. Justin was right. Somebody might come to take a look.

"Maybe I should throw him some cookies,"

Justin suggested.

"We need those for Marlon," Hartley told him. In a split second, he came up with an answer to the problem. "I know—Mom's meat loaf!"

Hartley pulled Justin out of sight behind the nearest tree. "If he can't see you, he won't bark. I'll be right back."

Then Hartley raced up the hill. He climbed through his bedroom window. He tiptoed down the hall to the kitchen and quietly opened the refrigerator.

Hartley grabbed the large piece of leftover meat loaf wrapped in foil. In minutes he was out the window, across the yard, and back down the hill again.

He shoved the silver package at Justin. "When the dog starts to bark, pull off hunks of this and throw them to him."

As long as he was chewing on a chunk of Mrs. Schroeder's meat loaf, the dog was quiet.

"See? He likes Mom's cooking—keep it up," Hartley said to Justin, snipping wire as fast as he could. At last he announced, "Just one more strand."

Snick—it was done! Hartley pulled the piece of fence aside. Now there was a hole big enough for Marlon to squeeze through.

The pig hung back, a little bewildered. It was the middle of the night, Hartley and Justin were acting kind of funny, and he wasn't used to walking out of his pen *through* the fence. Marlon whined softly and flopped his ears.

Hartley picked up one of the bags and pulled out a chocolate chip cookie. "Come on, Marlon," he coaxed. He rattled the bag. "Hear that? It's full of 'em. All these cookies are yours if you'll come out here. Mmm-mmm!" he added temptingly.

Marlon was wary. He snorted and poked his head coyly through the hole Hartley had snipped.

"That's right—come on," Hartley urged. "You'll be a lot better off out here with us."

Marlon grunted, bobbed his head as if to say yes, and finally pressed through the hole in the fence to the other side.

"Justin, he's free!" Hartley said, feeding Marlon a cookie and rubbing his back.

"Throw the rest of the meat loaf to the dog—let's get going!"

Hartley held out another chocolate chip cookie. "This way, Marlon. We're just taking a little stroll." Hartley whispered over his shoulder to Justin, "Don't forget the other bag of cookies."

The small procession headed by Hartley wound around the bottom of the hill in the direction of downtown Cedar Springs. "Marlon looks a lot bigger when he's standing out here with us than when he's on the other side of the fence," Justin observed uneasily. "What if he decides to run off? He weighs three times as much as we do, and how do you grab hold of a pig, anyway?" Marlon didn't really have a neck—his body sloped right into his head.

"Marlon'll go where the cookies go," Hartley replied confidently.

Cedar Springs was fast asleep. The boys kept Marlon well away from the glow of the street lamps, sticking to the shadows of trees and bushes edging the lawns. A couple of dogs barked halfheartedly. Otherwise, all was quiet, and Marlon followed Hartley as nicely as you please.

As the pig and the boys approached the center of town, however, Marlon stopped dead in his tracks. Like a bloodhound on a trail, he sniffed long and hard at the pink garbage can outside Mrs. Williams's Sweete Shoppe. Before the boys could stop him, Marlon knocked the garbage can over with a crash and jammed himself inside it up to his shoulders.

"P-pull it off!" Justin whispered sharply to Hartley.

"I'm trying!" Hartley hissed back. "It's stuck!"

Anyone who had been on Main Street at about one o'clock that Wednesday morning would have seen a strange sight: Hartley and Justin wrestling furiously with a pink garbage can on four legs. Luckily Main Street was deserted, although Justin kept glancing nervously over his shoulder as if he expected his father to appear at the door of the Handy Dandy.

Clang! Marlon ran into two more garbage cans with his metal head. *Bang!* He stumbled into a parking meter.

"I think that loosened it!" Hartley said. "Heave!"

Both boys tugged at the garbage can as hard as they could. It popped off the pig and

went rolling across Main Street, strewing empty ice cream containers and paper cups. Marlon was straddling the yellow stripe in the middle of the road, nibbling part of an ice cream cone someone had thrown out.

"We have to get him out of the street. What if a car comes?" Justin squeaked.

"Cookies, Marlon," Hartley said, holding out a fistful. He sounded calmer than he felt.

The boys hurried across Main Street, and Marlon trotted between them again, gobbling down cookies. His ears swiveled back and forth with interest and his hoofs skipped along the pavement like tap shoes. The pig was enjoying himself in the big outdoors.

In fact, he was enjoying himself almost too much. Not three blocks farther along, Marlon's keen nose picked up an attractive scent. This time it was the good things growing in the Owenses' yard.

Marlon zigged through their garden like a runaway Rototiller, rooting up all of the sweet potatoes and snatching tomatoes and beans as he plowed past. He snorted and squealed his excitement.

"Do you hear him?" Justin moaned. "Mr. Owens'll be out here with a shotgun any second!"

"Grab the potato plants!" Hartley directed.

Carrying armfuls of sweet potatoes, the boys lured the pig down the street and across the railroad tracks. From there it wasn't far to the dirt road to the Thompson place. The spooky old house couldn't have looked better to them.

After a long drink and a short wallow in the puddle in Cullen Creek, Marlon agreeably followed the boys right into the pen. Justin slammed the gate closed and collapsed against the fence.

"We did it!" Hartley declared. "My plan worked pretty well," he added.

"Are you kidding!" Justin replied indignantly. "We stole a pig, tore up a fence, threw trash all over Main Street, and wrecked a garden. About the only thing we didn't do is hold up the bank!"

"You'll feel better about things after you get some sleep," said Hartley. "Look at

Marlon—he's in hog heaven!"

The brown and white pig was chomping his way through the sweet potatoes, shuffling his feet and wiggling his tail contentedly.

"We saved a friend," Hartley said earnestly. "It was all worth it."

Justin just groaned.

7
A Few Things Go Wrong

At seven thirty that morning, Mrs. Schroeder tapped on the door of Hartley's bedroom. When her son opened a sleepy eye, she asked, "Hartley, have you seen your dad's wire cutters?"

"Oh, yeah." Hartley struggled out of bed and pulled the wire cutters out of the back pocket of the pants he'd left on the floor. He handed the cutters to his mother. "I just borrowed them for a minute last night."

"Hmm," his mother said. "You wouldn't know anything about that big piece of left-over meat loaf, would you?"

"I ate it," Hartley answered quickly. "Last night I woke up, and I was really hungry, so I ate the meat loaf."

"All right," his mother said. But she looked at him strangely.

Mrs. Schroeder became even more thoughtful later that morning when a Cedar Springs Sheriff's Department patrol car pulled up in front of the house. Sheriff Brooks himself climbed out and walked up the sidewalk to the front door.

"Morning, Mrs. Schroeder," the sheriff said. "Is Hartley around?"

"Good morning, Sheriff," Hartley's mom said. "He's just finishing his breakfast. Come right in."

When she showed Sheriff Brooks into the kitchen, Hartley put down the piece of toast he'd been eating and pushed his plate away. He had suddenly lost his appetite again.

"Morning, Hartley," the sheriff said. "I thought you might be able to help me."

"Yes, sir?" Hartley answered.

"Gus Albright's brown and white pig is missing," Sheriff Brooks told him.

"Oh?" said Hartley.

"Somebody cut a hole in the back fence at the Aquarama," the sheriff went on. "We noticed a dirt trail leading up the hill from the fence to your backyard. When we asked Gus about it, he said you and the Jones boy feed the pig through the back fence from time to time. I thought if the animal was loose, it might've come looking for you."

"Oh—no, sir," said Hartley. He was starting to feel a little queasy.

"A hole in the fence?" Mrs. Schroeder asked.

"That's right," replied Sheriff Brooks. "Looks like wire cutters were used on it."

"Hmm . . . " said Hartley's mother. "Can you tell us if you found any other clues?"

Sheriff Brooks shook his head. "Not really," he said. "There *was* a wadded-up ball of aluminum foil near the fence."

The tin foil from the meat loaf! Hartley thought. "But that could have been dropped days ago," the sheriff added.

The sheriff turned back to Hartley. "So you wouldn't have any idea where that pig might be?" he asked again.

"No, sir."

"Well, if you have any thoughts at all about it, let me know," Sheriff Brooks told him.

After Mrs. Schroeder walked the sheriff to the front door, she came back to the kitchen. She studied her youngest son quietly for a moment. "Hartley, do you have something you'd like to tell me?" she said at last.

"Um—I'm not too hungry. Must be all

that good meat loaf I ate last night," Hartley replied. "Hey, there's Justin! Gotta go, Mom." He leaped to his feet and scooted out the back door before she could say another word.

Justin was standing under the cypress tree. "I s-saw the sheriff leaving when I rode up the street," he said, his eyes wide.

"They're looking for Marlon," Hartley said in a low voice.

"G-great!" Justin muttered. "I knew this would happen!"

"Nothing's happened," Hartley said quickly. "We have other stuff to worry about— like getting some food to our pig!"

"H-how are we going to do that? The whole Cedar Springs Sheriff's Department'll be watching us!" cried Justin.

"We'll find a way," said Hartley.

And they did. They worked sneakily, and all day long on their bikes. Hartley raided his mother's garden, his grandmother's garden, and even his aunt's garden.

Justin scoured the store for anything that looked the least bit old, dented, or mashed: half-gallons of milk that were out of date, wilted vegetables, packages of cookies that were a little crushed.

Marlon ate whatever they gave him, and stamped his feet for more. By the middle of the afternoon, both boys were going through the town's garbage cans.

"Where have you been? Did somebody see you?" Justin asked, waiting at the pen for Hartley at the end of one trip.

"I spotted a patrol car on Main Street," Hartley answered. "I had to go the long way around." He unstrapped two trash bags he'd fastened to the back of his bike. "Stuff from behind the Springs Cafe," he explained.

Hartley poured the contents of one bag into Marlon's pen. The pig attacked the trash as though he hadn't already eaten fourteen times that day! It wasn't long before Marlon was looking up at Hartley and squealing pitifully for more.

"Doesn't he ever fill up?" Justin grumbled. "Hartley, we can't keep doing this! Dad's not going to have anything left in his store. Either somebody's going to see us, or we're going to run out of food. Or we'll just plain wear ourselves out."

Hartley dumped the second bag of garbage next to Marlon and watched the pig crunch his way through it. Hartley knew what Justin meant . . . but Marlon was such a nice pig. They couldn't give him up, no matter what!

"We'll figure something out," he promised.

Hartley made one more trip, late that afternoon. This time he was carrying a bottle of brown shoe polish he'd borrowed from his sister's room. He climbed into Marlon's pen and brushed it carefully over the white spot on Marlon's side.

"If anybody happens to come by here, you're just a plain, all-brown pig," Hartley told him, "not Gus Albright's famous spotted swimming pig. Remember that."

Marlon's eyes met Hartley's, and his lips curled in a grin.

At the Schroeders' supper table that night, Hap announced, "Somebody stole Gus Albright's pig."

"Yes," said Mrs. Schroeder. "Sheriff Brooks stopped by to tell us."

Hartley didn't look up—he just kept flattening down his mashed potatoes with his fork.

"It's all right," Hap went on. "The new one was ready to go, anyway." He nudged Hartley. "Did you see him dive today?"

"No," Hartley answered. He hadn't had time.

"Donna says he's doing just fine. She likes him better than the other one—not so rambunctious," Hap reported.

Good, Hartley thought. *Maybe they'll forget all about Marlon.* He raised his eyes to find his father looking right at him.

Mr. Schroeder had an expression on his face that startled Hartley. It was almost as though he knew what Hartley was going through, and he understood.

8
The Fire

Hartley's mother stopped him before he could get out of the house the next morning. "Hartley," she said, "it's your turn to mow the lawn."

"But I have to meet Justin," he protested. After a whole night with nothing to eat Marlon must be starving!

"You're not going anywhere until you've mowed the lawn," Mrs. Schroeder told him. "Justin will have to wait."

Hartley stamped out of the house. He'd pulled the mower from the garage to the driveway and was just starting it up when Justin arrived, out of breath.

"I've already been to the pen," he reported. "Marlon's so hungry, he's about ready to start chewing on the fence!"

"I knew it!" Hartley said apologetically.

"Mom said I had to do this first—it won't take that long."

"All I could find at the store to give him was some smelly old cheese," Justin said, adding glumly, "and the puddle in the creek is almost dried up. What'll we do then? Start hauling water to him too?"

"We'll try the Springs Cafe—see what they threw out after breakfast," Hartley said, refusing to sound as discouraged as his friend. "I found really good stuff there yesterday."

"Hartley, you'd better hurry up," Mrs. Schroeder called. "Look at that sky."

The heat was piling the clouds over Cedar Springs into a towering thunderhead.

"It might rain," Hartley said to Justin. "If it does, maybe the creek'll fill up. Then at least we won't have to worry about Marlon's water." This thought cheered Hartley. He gripped the starter cord on the mower. "Let me finish this dumb yard so we can get out of here."

He pulled hard and the mower roared to life. Justin sat down on the back steps to wait for him.

Hartley raced back and forth across the lawn, pushing the mower as though his life depended on it. He hadn't even finished the backyard when the first fat drops of rain began to fall.

"Come into the house, Hartley." His mother waved from the kitchen door. Justin was already inside.

But Hartley pretended he couldn't understand her over the noise of the mower. He wanted to be done with it and get over to Marlon's pen.

Cra-a-ack! A bolt of lightning zigzagged out of the sky not a mile away! A tremendous thunderclap followed fast on its heels. The sky turned a dark blue, and the light rain became a drenching downpour. Hartley was soaked before he could turn off the mower and get into the house.

"Dry yourself off and change out of those wet clothes," his mother ordered. She handed Hartley a big towel as he and Justin walked down the hall to his room.

Cra-a-ack! Boom! More lightning tore through the dark clouds over Cedar Springs.

One bolt struck so close to the house that both boys flinched.

"I hope Marlon isn't scared," Hartley said, thinking of one medium-size pig all alone behind the old Thompson house.

The boys sat down to wait it out. They watched the rain pour down the window, collect in puddles all over the Schroeders' backyard, and stream down the driveway.

Suddenly the downtown siren went off.

"It's not noon," said Justin. "Maybe the lightning started a brush fire!"

"This rain'll put it out pretty quick," was Hartley's opinion.

The siren blew again and again. Soon the clang of the Cedar Springs fire engine drifted up the hill.

"There goes the Volunteer Fire Department—I wonder where the fire is?" Hartley said.

The boys peered out of Hartley's window. The rain was slacking off, but they still couldn't see anything that looked like smoke.

Then the phone rang in the hall. Mrs. Schroeder picked it up. "Hello? . . . Oh, hello,

Edith . . . yes, we're fine out here . . . it's clearing up now. . . . What? The old Thompson place? Heavens—I hope they can put it out. I'm kind of surprised it hasn't burned down years before this!"

The boys didn't wait to hear anything more. They were out the door and on their bikes before Hartley's mother could hang up the phone.

"At least Marlon's pen is on the other side of the creek from the Thompson house. He should be safe enough from the fire," Hartley said.

The storm had faded to a sprinkle as the boys sped toward downtown Cedar Springs. Now that the sky had cleared, they could see the smoke. It surged like thick gray foam above their pig's hideaway.

"You think all these people are going to the fire?" Justin asked as they pedaled up Main Street. A line of trucks and cars stretched clear across the railroad tracks.

"Must be," Hartley answered. "There's nothing else for them to look at over there."

"But what if somebody sees Marlon?"

"I don't think anyone can get close enough to see him. Don't you hear that?" The gurgle of water was so loud it muffled the noise of the traffic. "Cullen Creek is running," Hartley said. "Nobody'll be able to cross it for hours."

Then Hartley told Justin about the brown shoe polish disguise. "If someone happens to look across the creek and sees a pig in the pen," Hartley explained, "it'll be an all-brown pig he's seeing."

Justin had to admit—some of Hartley's ideas were inspired.

There were cars parked all along the dirt road that curved toward the old Thompson place. Everybody was at the fire—the Cedar Springs Volunteer Fire Department, of course, but also Hap and the guys in the highway department, Mr. Schroeder in his electrician's overalls, Justin's mother on her way home from the hairdresser, lots of kids the boys knew from school, Sheriff Brooks, even . . .

"Gus Albright!" Justin choked. Gus was standing to one side in his white cowboy hat.

"No big deal," Hartley said. He had taken

a quick look across the creek at Marlon's hideout. He was sure that with all the noise and confusion no one would even notice the pen, much less the pig. Now he was giving his full attention to the enormous stream of water the fire fighters had aimed at the Thompson house. As the water pounded the burning boards it turned instantly into great clouds of steam.

Over the hiss of the rising steam, however, the boys suddenly heard someone shout, "There's a pig in the creek!"

Both boys turned as one, their eyes on the swirling muddy water, their hearts sinking. As they feared, it was Marlon.

Hartley hadn't counted on the appeal a big crowd held for the pig, and now he realized this was a serious oversight. To Marlon, all these people gathered around meant he should do the thing he liked best (after eating): perform. So he'd shoved at the fence until it came down and then charged into the swiftly running water of Cullen Creek. Now he was climbing out into the backyard of the Thompson house, looking around for his after-swim snack with an expectant smile on his face.

"Brooks!" Gus Albright yelled. "Here's my missing pig!"

Hartley was going to have to do some fast talking. He raced over to the dripping pig with Justin right behind him. "Sheriff," Hartley said hastily, "Marlon was brown and white. This pig is just brown."

"He's right, Gus," Sheriff Brooks agreed.

Unfortunately, just then little Clyde Davison slipped and fell into Cullen Creek. He splashed and thrashed as the water pulled him farther away from the bank.

"Help!" his mother screamed. "I can't swim! Clyde's going to drown!"

When Marlon heard this, it was as if he were getting his cue at the Aquarama. He didn't hesitate. He dove straight into the rushing water.

Marlon gave a perfect performance. In seconds he had his teeth in the back of little Clyde's shirt. Avoiding the sticks and branches whirling down the creek, Marlon tugged the little boy to safety.

"I don't know what happened to his white spot, but that's my pig or my name isn't Gus

Albright!" growled Gus Albright. He glared suspiciously at Hartley and Justin.

Sheriff Brooks turned to look at them too. "Well, boys?" he said.

9
Marlon's New Career

Before Hartley could think of anything to say, Mrs. Davison cried, "The pig saved my baby!"

A fire fighter waded into the creek to take little Clyde from Marlon. The pig scrambled up onto the bank to a big round of applause from the Volunteer Fire Department and all of the onlookers. Marlon shook himself off and looked around hopefully for his reward.

"Well, I guess everything has worked out," Mr. Albright said to Sheriff Brooks. "It's only Thursday—I can still get Marlon to the Paleyville auction this week."

"No!" Hartley shouted. He threw himself at Marlon protectively. Even Justin drew himself up to scowl at Mr. Albright.

Then a voice boomed out behind them. "You're going to auction a pig who saved a

little boy's life? Turn a hero into bacon bits?"
It was Mr. Schroeder, and he said it loud
enough for a lot of people to hear. He gave
Hartley and Justin a sympathetic wink.

"What?" Mrs. Davison said. She had been
hugging Clyde, and laughing and crying.
"You can't do that!" she told Gus Albright.

"Afraid not," agreed Frank Wallace, the
Cedar Springs fire chief. "I'm going to rec-
ommend this pig for a medal from the American Humane Society! It would be pretty em-
barrassing to have to admit that the lifesaver
was now sliced ham."

"I'm not going to feed *two* pigs," Gus Albright snapped. "And what about the money
I'll lose by *not* selling him?"

"I think Marlon might make a good mas-
cot for the Cedar Springs Fire Department,"
Mr. Schroeder suggested to the fire chief.
"You'd be the only fire department in the
United States with a lifesaving pig for a mas-
cot. You'd probably get written up in *People*
magazine. It'd be good advertising for the
Aquarama, too, Gus," Mr. Schroeder added.
"After all, you trained him."

"I'd like to take the pig on," said Fire Chief Wallace. "I could feed him from the farm." When he wasn't putting out fires, Mr. Wallace was a farmer. "But the volunteers can't afford to buy him right now—we need new fire hoses."

Sheriff Brooks spoke up. "Gus, it might be nice if you donated Marlon to the fire department. You have plenty of reason to be grateful to them—they saved you a lot of money last year, putting out that blaze at the Aquarama."

Mr. Albright looked a little sulky at first, but then he gave in. "Okay," he said to the fire chief, "the pig is yours."

"Yay!" Hartley and Justin shouted. They hugged Marlon's fat sides while the pig wriggled with pleasure and snorted in their ears.

"Not so fast, boys," Sheriff Brooks said. "I have a feeling you may have had something to do with that hole in the fence. How are you going to make it up to Mr. Albright?"

Hartley and Justin had been working at the Aquarama for a week. They mowed the lawn, cleaned up the trash scattered by the paying customers, and swept the walks and the auditorium.

"Two hours every day for the rest of the summer!" Justin grumbled. "What a great vacation!" He yanked a weed out of the sidewalk. "I guess it could be worse —like jail!"

Justin looked at his friend. "Hartley? Hartley!"

Hartley hadn't heard a word Justin had said. He was leaning on his broom, still as a statue. It was the first show of the day, and Hartley's eyes were on the brown and white pig standing poised at the end of the Aquarama diving board.

Suddenly the smooth body shot into the air. The pig tucked his head and slipped cleanly into the bright water of the pool. The crowd applauded loudly.

Hartley turned to Justin with a funny look on his face. "He's an awfully good little diver," Hartley said. "He seems like a very nice pig, too," he added. "I think we should make friends with him. You never know. . . ."

"Oh, *no*!" cried Justin Jones.

About the Author

SUSAN SAUNDERS really likes pigs. "Pigs are neither dirty, nor stupid, nor lazy," she says. "It's true that they lie around in the mud, but they do it to cool off, not to be piggy. They'd be just as happy lying in a nice clean pool. Pigs can learn to open locks and—in the court of Louis XI—to dance. They enjoy music and television.

"A few years ago a pig won an award from the American Humane Association for saving a retarded child from drowning. That and the old saying, 'Don't wish for anything too hard, because you just might get it,' gave me the idea for this story. National Pig Day," she adds, "is March first."

Susan Saunders grew up in Texas and now lives in New York.

About the Illustrator

GAIL OWENS has illustrated many funny novels for young readers. She lives and works in Rock Tavern, New York.